This Little Tiger book belongs to:

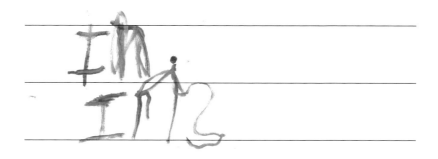

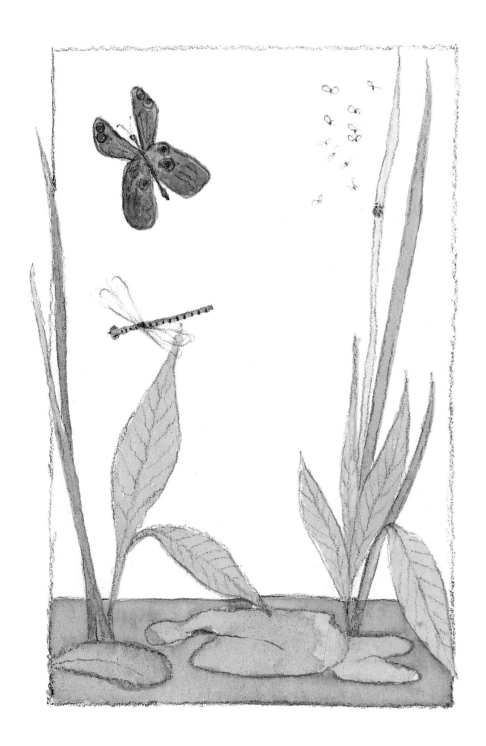

For Simon, Alison and Laura
~ A H B

For Maxim and Olivia
~ E H

LITTLE TIGER PRESS
An imprint of Magi Publications
1 The Coda Centre, 189 Munster Road, London SW6 6AW
www.littletigerpress.com

First published in Great Britain 1998
This Bookstart edition published 2008

A CIP catalogue record for this book is available
from the British Library

Printed in China

2 4 6 8 10 9 7 5 3 1

A DUCK SO SMALL

A H Benjamin
Elisabeth Holstien

LITTLE TIGER PRESS
London

Duffle was a very small duck and,
because of his size, all the other ducks
laughed at him.

"A duck so small can do nothing at all!"
they jeered.
"I may be small," thought Duffle sadly,
"but there must be *something* I can do."
He wondered what it could be.

Duffle looked around and noticed
Kingfisher perching on a reed.
He was just about to say hello,
when . . .

. . . Kingfisher suddenly took off and dived, straight as an arrow, into the water.

"Kingfisher is small," thought Duffle, "but see how well he dives. Perhaps I could do that, too."

"Look what I can do!" Duffle
called out to the other ducks.
He flew high into the air . . .

. . . and came down again
like a dropped stone.

Duffle hit the water so hard that he nearly
bounced off it!

"Ha, ha, ha, what did we say?" cried the other
ducks. "A duck so small can do nothing at all!"

Poor Duffle felt very foolish.
He climbed out onto the
riverbank, wondering
what to do next.

Duffle saw Heron, standing perfectly still on one leg in the shallow water.

"What good balance she has," thought Duffle. "Perhaps I could do that, too."

"Look what I can do!"
Duffle called, as he
stood on one leg with
his wings spread out.

He wobbled this way
and that and . . .

. . . landed flat on his beak.

"Ha, ha, ha, what did we say?" laughed the other ducks. "A duck so small can do nothing at all!"

Duffle crept off into the shade of a tree so that
the other ducks wouldn't notice his blushes.
Tap, tap, tap, went a sound above his head.

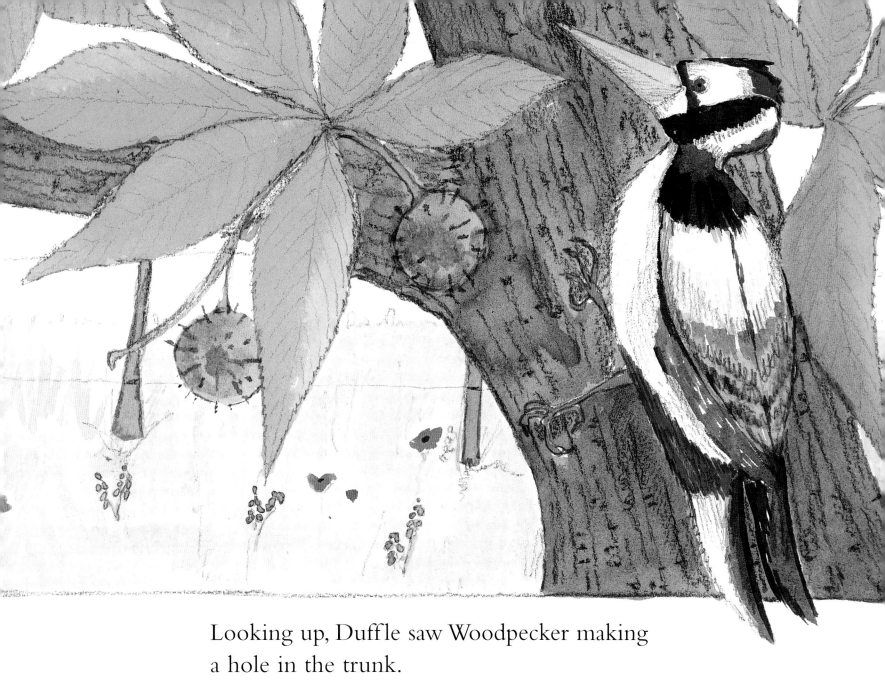

Looking up, Duffle saw Woodpecker making
a hole in the trunk.
"What a strong beak he has," thought the
little duck. "Perhaps I could bore a hole, too."

"Look what I can do!" Duffle called out to the other ducks. He flew up into the tree and perched on a thick branch. *Peck, peck, peck,* he went at the wood. "Oops," he cried as he lost his balance. Duffle toppled from the branch and . . .

. . . fell to the ground.

"Ha, ha, ha, what did we say?" cackled the other
ducks. "A duck so small can do nothing at all!"

All the ducks were paddling and splashing in the river, but poor Duffle decided to hide in the rushes until they left. That way he wouldn't have to listen to their sniggering.

"I'm good at nothing," he thought. "I'm just a small, useless duck." And a tear rolled down his beak.

For a long time, Duffle could still hear those ducks quacking with laughter. It seemed as though they would never leave.

"I'll stay here just a bit longer till they get tired of it," he thought. But as he listened, he realised something.

The ducks weren't laughing at him.
They were quacking in alarm!

Duffle paddled over to see what all the fuss
was about. It seemed that a duckling had got
stuck in a tiny hole in the riverbank.

"Oh, please get him out," begged the duckling's
mother.

"We will," said the other ducks, but it was no good.
They were just too big to squeeze into the hole.

All except for Duffle.

"Let *me* try," he said and, because he was so small, he was able to reach right in.

It didn't take him long to
rescue the trapped
duckling.

"Good old Duffle!" cried one duck.

   "None of us could have done that," said another.

   "A duck so small *can* be useful after all!"
quacked a third.

"Oh, it was nothing," blushed Duffle. And,
though he was only a little duck, he felt bigger
and stronger than them all.

You'll go quackers for these Little Tiger books!

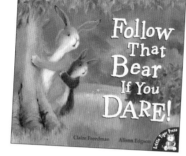

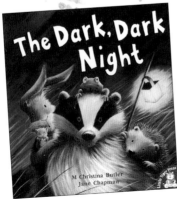

For information regarding any of the above titles
or for our catalogue, please contact us:
Little Tiger Press, 1 The Coda Centre,
189 Munster Road, London SW6 6AW
Tel: 020 7385 6333 Fax: 020 7385 7333
E-mail: info@littletiger.co.uk
www.littletigerpress.com